**WARNING!**

You may get a case of

(SUDDEN SICK PANTS)

when you hear about the gigantic
robotic-chicken's bum later in this
story. But it's not my fault.
I had to do what I did to protect
THE BIGGEST SECRET EVER!

COMING SOON FROM

JOSHIE LEFERS

BOOK 2
The Rise of the Bread Baby

BOOK 3
Chasing the Cannibal Clone

BOOK 4
The Brain-chip Farter Starter

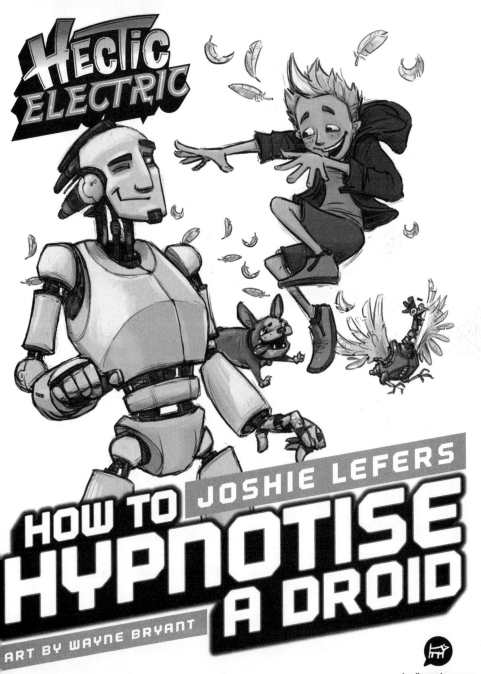

HECTIC ELECTRIC

HOW TO JOSHIE LEFERS HYPNOTISE A DROID

ART BY WAYNE BRYANT

hardie grant EGMONT

How to Hypnotise a Droid
published in 2017 by
Hardie Grant Egmont
Ground Floor, Building 1, 658 Church Street
Richmond, Victoria 3121, Australia
www.hardiegrantegmont.com

A CiP record for this title is available from the
National Library of Australia.

Illustration by Wayne Bryant
Cover design by Kristy Lund–White
Internal design and typesetting by Pooja Desai

Printed in Australia by McPhersons Printing Group,
Maryborough, Victoria, an accredited ISO AS/NZS
14001 Environmental Management System printer.

1 3 5 7 9 10 8 6 4 2

To Dad.
Thanks for being the most wonderful
creative inspiration a boy called Joshie
could ever ask for!

CHAPTER 1

'There's never a dull day in the life of Joshie Hectic,' Dad used to say. Then we got hit by lightning on the beach. That's how I got the silver lightning bolt in my hair. And *that's* how I got nicknamed **HECTIC ELECTRIC**.

Well that, and because I was always doing **HECTIC** stuff like chasing sharks on my surfboard.

But then something happened that you'll never believe. Something WILD. Something HUGE. Something that added **A MILLION VOLTS** of **HECTIC ELECTRIC** to my life!

It all started one morning, when I was eating muesli with soy milk **(YUCK!)**. Someone started banging on our apartment door like crazy.

I knew it was probably Crazy Cat

Granny from next door, because my dog
Frenchy was **NEXT LEVEL** barking.

He has a sixth sense for when she and
her cats are around.

I don't know how many cats Crazy Cat Granny has, but the Ginger Nut twins (who live opposite) say it's forty. Maybe including some dead ones in shoeboxes.

Of course, I *never* believe the Ginger Nut twins.

I heard Mum open the front door. Sure enough, it was Crazy Cat Granny.

'This HUGE box came for you!' she cackled. 'What's in it? Better open it before my kitties get there first!'

My ears pricked up. Huge box? We *hardly ever* get deliveries. I craned my neck to see, and could just make out a long cardboard box in our doorway. There were at least two cats already meowing and scratching at it.

'And why does it say **TOP SECRET**?' asked Crazy Cat Granny.

At that, I sprang out of my chair. We definitely never had any **TOP SECRET** deliveries. Frenchy was still barking like a maniac as I sprinted to the front door.

'Oh, it's arrived,' Mum said, dragging the enormous box inside. 'Yes, thank you, Crazy — um, Glenda.' She shut the door on our nosy neighbour and her mangy cats.

'Joshie,' Mum added, pulling the box into the kitchen, 'stop that dog barking or we'll get a visit from the landlord.'

'No barking,' I told Frenchy quickly, 'or **MR MOUSTACHE MAN** will make you sleep on the balcony.'

Mr Moustache Man is our landlord. **He HATES** dogs more than **I HATE** soy milk.

Then I turned to Mum. 'What's in the box? WHAT'S IN THE BOX?'

'Calm down, Joshie,' Mum said. 'The box is for you, but it's **TOP SECRET** so you can't open it till I get home from work.'

My jaw dropped. 'But MUM —'

'DO NOT OPEN THE BOX,' she said. 'Not till I get home tonight. Promise?'

'Okaaaaaay,' I said.

But this was exactly like telling the chicken not to cross the road. I NEVER follow instructions. I just HAD to know what was inside.

I knew Mum was about to leave for work, because she did the **exact same** things in the **exact same** order, as usual:

1. She put on her lab coat.
2. She took her keys from the hook by the door and spun them around her right pointy finger three times.
3. She pressed on the lids of each of the ten pens in the top pocket of her lab coat.

If you didn't already know it, you'll soon see:

MUM'S GOT LOADS OF

WEIRD

LITTLE HABITS.

The other thing you should know about Mum? I have to remind her what *normal* mums do before they leave for work. And I pretty much have to remind her EVERY day.

I said, 'Muuuum! Aren't you forgetting something?'

She looked at me blankly. Then it dawned on her. 'Oh, sorry!' she said, and strode back into the room to give me an awkward hug. She planted a big kiss on my forehead.

I rolled my eyes and smiled, like Dad and I used to when Mum was awks about stuff.

'That's what you get when you marry a mad scientist,' Dad would always joke.

'Have a good day at school,' Mum said.
'Oh hang on, when is your big painting due?'

'Today,' I groaned loudly. 'But I don't want to talk about it.'

We had to do a painting for art, and mine was a **DISASTER**. Everyone else in class had almost finished theirs, but I kept having to paint white over all my previous attempts because they **SUCKED**.

'What's your painting of?' asked Mum.

'A snowman in a snow storm,' I said with a straight face.

But Mum didn't get it. **As usual.** 'That sounds great,' she said.

I sighed. What made it worse was that the Ginger Nut twins were doing family portraits and they kept telling everyone theirs were **masterpieces**. The suck-ups even took their paintings home to keep working on them. **SUPER SUCK-UPS!**

The twins are called Nut (short for Hazelnut) and Ginger, and they are RIDICULOUSLY annoying. Yep, I like **soy milk** more than I like the Ginger Nut twins.

Mum planted another kiss on my forehead, way too close to my eye. 'Just paint whatever is in your heart,' she said. 'Remember you've got this big box to look forward to. I'll try and get home around the time you do.'

'Sure you will,' I said, knowing she wouldn't be home till dinnertime. **As usual.**

Mum gave me a stern look. 'Well, since you scared off the last babysitter, I'm going to have to,' she said.

I can't believe Mum was still angry about that. What was the big deal? All I'd done was tie a few bedsheets to our balcony rail.

It wasn't MY fault the babysitter thought Frenchy and I had run away. And it wasn't MY fault the babysitter got soaking wet looking for us during a thunderstorm ...

... while Frenchy and I were drinking hot chocolate in front of the heater.

'Right, I'm off to work,' Mum said. 'Just make sure you get to school on time. I don't want another note from Mr Trunkface.'

As soon as Mum shut the front door behind her, I jumped up and ran over to the **TOP SECRET** box.

First, I peered at it from every angle. It was a normal cardboard box, but it was **LOOOONG**. Almost as long as our kitchen table. Frenchy was sniffing all around it. 'What's inside, Frenchy?' I asked.

He gave a little whimper and started pawing at the box. But I couldn't understand what he was saying, because the only French word I know is **cROISSANT.**

I was curious, but there were at least **three** *quite* good reasons why I shouldn't open the box:

1. Mum had told me not to (and if anything went wrong I'd be in **BIG FAT TROUBLE**).

2. Last time I opened something from Mum's work when I wasn't meant to, I ended up getting chased down the street by a hologram of a lion.

3. I had to get to school on time to finish my painting (or Mr Trunkface would make me write lines for the rest of my life).

The problem was, Mum had said,

'DO NOT OPEN THE BOX'

but all I heard was, '**open the box**'.

See, I have a really serious disease called

Selective Hearing.

Selective Hearing makes it **VERY** hard

to hear things that are said about homework

and brushing teeth and vegetables. But

weirdly you can still hear when dessert is

ready or the end-of-school bell rings.

And so carefully — CAREFULLY — I peeled back the tiniest corner of cardboard to look inside. Just a *little* corner. Nothing Mum would notice. In red writing, I saw the words:

TOP SECRET

ROBOTICS INSTITUTE
AUTHORISED PERSONNEL ONLY

Which basically meant *not* me. It meant Mum. She's the boss at the Robotics Institute, which is why she had to be the one to open the box.

Maybe if I hadn't seen the **BIG RED BUTTON**, I would have stopped right there. Maybe I would have just gone to school.

But the button said **'PRESS TO OPEN'** and I *really* wanted to. I know I just told you I don't follow instructions, but I do follow **COOL ONES!**

I moved closer to get a better look. Suddenly, a **bright light** came on. Frenchy started barking. 'Stop that!' I said, holding him back by his collar. 'You'll get us in trouble with **MR MOUSTACHE MAN**.'

I just *had* to open the box now. I mean, there was a bright light AND a big red button.

And the button said, **'PRESS TO OPEN'**. It didn't say, **'WAIT UNTIL YOUR MUM GETS HOME, WHICH WILL BE LATE LIKE ALWAYS'**.

PLUS I had started to get that funny feeling inside my stomach. I call it **THE ITCH**. I always get **THE ITCH** before I do something exciting.

I leant forwards. My finger hovered over the button, getting closer, closer, closer. Frenchy started barking again.

Just then a voice came from inside the box. **'DO NOT PRESS THE BUTTON!'**

CHAPTER 2

I nearly jumped out of my hoodie.

'STRIKE ME DOWN!' I yelped.

I looked around but there was no-one else

in the room. My heart was pulsing like a

super-charge of electricity. Frenchy started

growling.

'Are you talking to me?' I asked the box.

A whirring noise came from inside the box. Then the voice said: 'I can tell from your voice patterns that you are Joshie Hectic. Therefore, the answer to your question is YES.'

Now I was beginning to feel **freaked**. Was there a person in there? But the voice didn't sound human. It sounded electronic, like Mum's phone when she asked it a question.

But Mum's phone didn't actually know what I was *doing*. And it definitely didn't know what I was *thinking* about doing next.

This was getting **HECTIC!**

There was a whirring noise again. 'Please stand back. Instructions have been given,' said the electronic voice. 'This box is not to be opened until your mother is home.'

'I'm not even near it!' I lied.

'My infrared sensor reads body heat. You are 12 centimetres from the button,' said the electronic voice. **'Therefore I conclude you are planning to open the box.'**

By now, Frenchy was going crazy.

He was racing around, barking and pawing at the box. I was about to tell him to stop when I felt THE ITCH again. This time THE ITCH gave me an idea that was probably even better than Nutella and popcorn toast.

'Frenchy, come here,' I said.

I said this in the voice I usually use when I want a cuddle. Frenchy looked at me with his big brown eyes and for a moment I felt bad. I wasn't going to cuddle him. I had something VERY different in mind.

I picked him up and took his right front paw in my hand. Then I leant towards the box.

The button glowed and the electronic voice warned, AGAIN, 'Do not press the button.'

'I won't,' I said.

I would never disobey Mum AND a mysterious voice by pressing that button, right? But no one had said anything about **Frenchy!**

I placed Frenchy's paw on the button.

Then three things happened very quickly.

1. The lid opened super-fast, like an automatic door **with a jet engine!**

2. An eerie fog wafted from the box.

3. Frenchy did the world's stinkiest fear fart (you can guess what that is).

As Frenchy and I
watched, a kind of super-
fancy metal-man sat up
inside the box. He placed
one hand on each side
and pulled himself
up to standing.

Then he stepped
smoothly out of the
box and onto our
kitchen floor.
He was covered
in a kind of white
metal, except for his

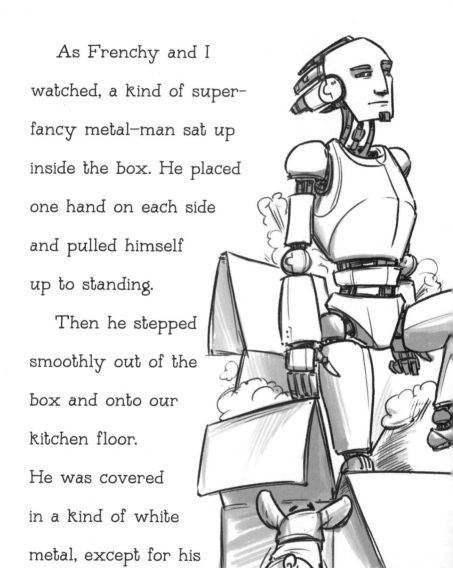

joints, which glowed blue.

You wouldn't believe the **HECTIC**-tech

of it! It was like a super-charged car engine,

with the metal cogs of a clock from the future,

combined with the tiny parts from inside a

computer.

'Wow! What are you?' I gasped, circling the strange metal-man thingy.

'To be precise,' he said, 'I'm an artificially intelligent, shape-shifting droid.'

My jaw dropped. **'Awesomeness!'** I said. Because you know what a droid is, right?

IT'S A ROBOT THAT LOOKS AND ACTS LIKE A HUMAN.

CHAPTER 3

Can you believe it?! A real-life droid! It was
the coolest thing that had happened to me
in ages — although to be fair, the arrival of a
strange droid in our home wasn't as surprising
as you might think.

Once you get to know my crazy scientist mum, you'll understand that anything is possible. Anything except **normal**, that is.

A thousand thoughts flew through my head all at once. 'Are you a new breed of cyber human?' I asked. 'Or on a secret mission for the CIA, or the FBI or something?!'

The droid looked at me. 'Negative. I am part of a secret program called R.A.D. D.A.D.'

'Oh,' I said, a little disappointed. That didn't sound so cool. 'What does that stand for?'

'It is not standing for anything,' the droid said. 'It is not sitting for anything either. It means Robotic Assistance Droid for Daytime and After-hours Duties.'

Is it just me or does that sound like some sort of **droidy babysitter?** I know I've scared off my share of babysitters, but that's only because I **don't** need a babysitter anymore. I *am* ten years old, after all.

'I am programmed to look after you when your mother is at work,' the droid added.

'So, like, all the time?' I said.

'Negative. There are 7 days in a week. That is 168 hours or 1080 minutes —'

'Chill out,' I said, rolling my eyes. 'I didn't *actually* mean all the time.'

'I am not overheating,' the droid said.

I started giggling. I mean, the droid was pretty awesome but he was a total geek, too. 'Oh man, we **have** to work on your personality,' I told him.

'This is my generic conversation program. I have 257 possible personalities to choose from,' the droid said.

'Could you just be a bit cooler?'

'Affirmative. How many ice-cubes would you like me to produce?'

I rolled my eyes at Frenchy. If I was being my usual **HECTIC** self, I would have tested out all 257 personalities straight away. He needed a much **cooler** personality.

But there would be plenty of time for that. First I wanted to see what the droid could actually **do**.

'What has Mum programmed you to do?' I asked.

'I am programmed to be your babysitter,' the droid said. 'And it is breakfast time. Would you like some *toast* –?'

Frenchy started barking at the word **toast**. Oops!

'Sorry, Frenchy,' I said quickly. 'We don't use the **T-word** here, okay?' I told the droid. 'Mum brought home a high-tech toaster a few weeks ago and it fell in love with Frenchy.

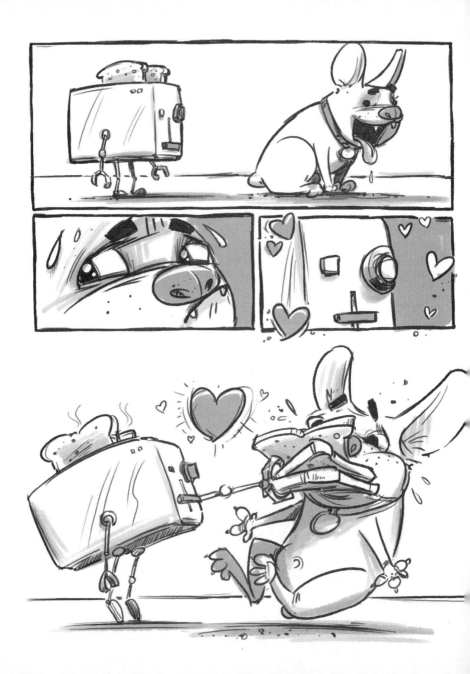

It fed him **toast** until he was so fat he got stuck in the dog door.'

Frenchy barked even louder.

'Besides,' I added, 'I've already eaten. But what are you making for lunch?'

'Checking pre-programming,' said the droid. He started making a noise like a games console loading a new game. 'Your mother has a pre-command for vegan stew for Tuesday school lunches,' the droid informed me.

Yuckkk! My stomach squirmed. Then I saw the time and realised I was going to be late for school. 'Oh no!' I groaned. 'The bell goes in twelve minutes. Even when I run my fastest, I can only get there in fourteen. Which means I'm going to be late for art class, and my painting is due today — and it's still just a white canvas!'

'I will be taking you to school and bringing you home,' the droid answered. 'That is my first priority. Please get your schoolbag while I create your goggles.'

'GOGGLES?' I said. 'What do I need goggles for?'

'They will protect your eyes when we travel at *MEGASPEEDS*. Creating your googles now.'

I didn't know what *MEGASPEEDS*

were, but I could hardly wait to find out.

The droid's eyes started spinning in their sockets and made a sound like when Mum uses the blender to make her horrible kale and broccoli smoothies. Then two clear silicon circles popped from the droid's eyes and into his hands. 'Your goggles,' he said.

I put them on. It felt like they were trying to suck my eyeballs out of my skull. 'You mean eyeball-suckers!' I corrected him.

'Eight minutes and 54 seconds until school time,' the droid said. 'Calculating required **MEGASPEED** to arrive on time. Please choose your mode onscreen:

- **GREEN TREE FROG**
- **AFRICAN CHEETAH**
- **KILLER BEE**
- **MEXICAN DONKEY**

I gaped at him. 'You mean, using one of these will get me to school in time?'

'That is correct,' the droid said.

THE ITCH in my tummy was going crazy again. It was like I was being tickled by a thousand spider-monkey fingers. I didn't know what would happen, but I had a feeling it was going to be **TOTAL AWESOMENESS!**

'AFRICAN CHEETAH mode,' I said immediately. But then I thought about how cool it would be to fly. 'No, wait! Let's go for KILLER BEE.'

The droid's white-metal body began to shift. Which meant I was about to find out exactly what a shape-shifting droid does!

All at once, his legs started to bend out at strange angles. His eyes blew out like giant bubble-gum bubbles until they were the size of bowling balls.

KILLER-BEE MODE

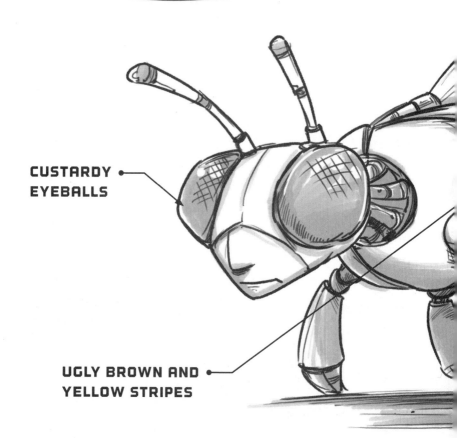

CUSTARDY
EYEBALLS

UGLY BROWN AND
YELLOW STRIPES

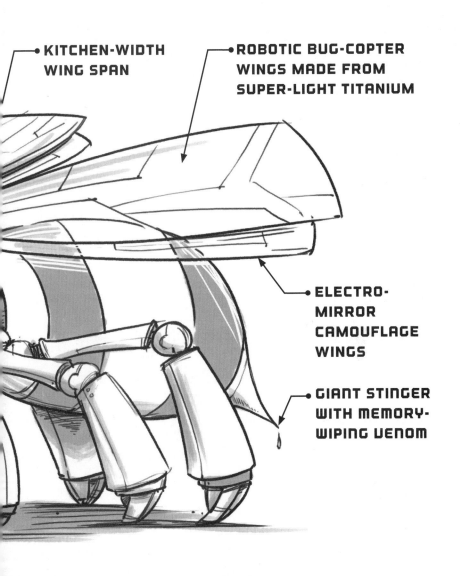

KITCHEN-WIDTH WING SPAN

ROBOTIC BUG-COPTER WINGS MADE FROM SUPER-LIGHT TITANIUM

ELECTRO-MIRROR CAMOUFLAGE WINGS

GIANT STINGER WITH MEMORY-WIPING VENOM

'**BUUUUUUZZZZZ** ... I calculate we have a 98.9 per cent chance of remaining undetected by curiouzzz neighbourzzz in apartmentzzz 22, 23 and 25 if we leave via the balcony,' the droid said in his electronic killer-bee voice.

'Good idea,' I said, although I had no idea how he knew about Crazy Cat Granny, the Ginger Nut twins and **MR MOUSTACHE MAN**.

Then I realised something else. 'We need to keep you **TOP SECRET** right? Which means we can't arrive at school in front of all the kids either.'

'Affirmative,' buzzed the droid. 'If anybody findzzz out about me, I will be recycled. And your mother will need a new job.'

I gulped. It was bad enough that I'd taken the droid out of the box when I'd promised not to. But making Mum lose her job at the Robotics Institute? That would destroy her. And now that Dad was gone, if Mum lost her job we'd be out on the street. But since she would probably kill me anyway, maybe becoming homeless was the least of my worries.

'We'd better land at the school's back gate,' I said. 'Nobody goes in that way.'

'Affirmative,' said the droid. 'The back gate lowerzzz our chance of detection by 78 per cent. But you must stay on my back until I confirm that it'zzz safe to dismount. Nobody will be able to see uzzz if my electro-mirror camouflage panelzzz are activated.' Then he moved one of his wings so the light in the lounge room bounced from one of his panels right into my eye.

I cheered. 'An electro-mirror? That's pretty **HECTIC ELECTRIC!** We'll be invisible?'

'Affirmative,' said the droid. 'But Joshie, we need to leave in the next 10.6 secondzzz to arrive on time. Please climb on.'

I didn't need to be asked twice. I grabbed

my bag and started scrambling onto his back.

'STOP! STOP!' the robotic bee buzzed.

'NEVER put your **HANDZZZZ** near my

STINGER!'

I'm not going to lie to you, I juMPed when

I saw the **giant** stinger dripping with

KILLER-BEE VENOM.

'Would that kill me?' I asked, springing

back.

'No. I am programmed to not endanger

humanzzz. It only createzzz a deep coma.'

'Um, okay.' I wondered if I should have

chosen GREEN TREE FROG instead.

'Climb onto my back from the base of my wingzzz, please,' he buzzed.

Steering clear of his stinger, I clambered onto his hairy bee back. The wings were made out of super-light titanium.

'**BUZZZZZZ!** Hold on to my eyelidzzz with your handzzz,' the robotic bee said. 'Commencing take-off.'

'If you say so,' I said, feeling funny about putting my hands into his eyes.

Gross. It was like dipping my hands into bowls of custard. Oh, and **double gross!** His eyelids flicked back so I could see the insides of them. Talk about wanting to puke.

Then suddenly ...

'STRIKE ME DOWN!' I yelled.

The next thing I knew we were rising into the

air. It was the best feeling ever!

Woooowah!!!

ahhhh!!!!!

Anyone normal would have thought I was crazy flying on a giant robotic killer bee. But what do normal people know, anyway?

CHAPTER 4

My hair was suddenly brushing past the ceiling lights. Before I knew it, we were buzzing through the open balcony door as Frenchy barked a very confused goodbye.

We were off! I could smell the salty sea air as we flew high towards the Esplanade.

With a high-powered **_WHOOOSHHHH_**
we were flying over the streets towards school.

I looked down and saw Ginger and Nut's
dad driving them to school.

Normally, the twins waved and giggled at
me as I walked to school and their dad *drove*
them. In his convertible Porsche.

It just wasn't fair. They still had their dad
but mine was gone, gone, gone. Sure, I still
had Mum, but ... well, she always left early
for work. And came home late.

I had to admit that I still felt sorry
for myself, even after all this time.

But now? Here I was, zooming over the Porsche at **MEGASPEEDS** only a giant robotic killer bee could go!

'Yeeehaaaaaaa!!! Giddy-up, Killer!' I shouted as we rose above the palm trees lining the Esplanade.

'Please increase your hand grip by 37 per cent to retain full balance in the ocean wind,' the bee buzzed through his bum speaker.

It was all going great. That is, until we flew over the beach where Dad used to teach me to surf. The exact same beach where Dad and I had been struck by lightning almost two years ago.

I touched my silver lightning-streak of hair, feeling weird all of a sudden. Even the doctors couldn't explain why Dad was killed by the lightning, when all I got was a new hairdo.

My throat felt kind of tight, and my eyes had started watering. It must have been because we were travelling at **MEGASPEEDS**. Or maybe the goggles weren't working.

It wasn't because I was crying about Dad. **Not. One. Bit.** I started to feel sick in the stomach.

'WE NEED TO LAND!' I yelled at the droid. 'I'm not feeling well.'

But the robotic bee kept flying. 'Estimating 1 minute and 35 secondzzz to arrival,' he announced.

Maybe he couldn't hear me. By now, my goggles were full of salty water. My eyes were stinging. I ripped off the goggles and squeezed my eyes closed.

'Descending towardzzz the back gate of the school now,' said the robotic bee. 'Once we land, my electro-mirror camouflage will drop away. I will become visible again.'

I opened my eyes. Beneath us I could just make out the school.

My heart skipped. A Porsche was pulling

into the back gate.

Oh, no. It was the twins! They must have gone to the back gate so they could carry in their paintings.

'Don't land!' I shouted to the bee.

But my words were swallowed by the wind.

This was a disaster. If the twins saw me landing at school on a gigantic robotic killer bee, they'd tell everyone.

I leant over, trying to spot somewhere else to land, when suddenly I lost my grip.

I was hanging on by a single gooey eyelid, but the custardy eyeball was just too slippery.

I was f a l l l i n n n g!

The funny thing (if there's *anything* funny about dying at ten years old) was that even though I was falling at top speed from the back of a giant robotic bee, everything was going in slow-motion.

I could see Ginger and Nut getting out of the car with their paintings. They were heading through the back gate. I could see kids lining up on the other side of the building. I could see Mr Trunkface unlocking our classroom.

So not only was I about to die, but I was probably going to be late as well.

'Yahhahahhgagahhahhahahhh!' I cried, as I plummeted towards breaking every bone in my body.

I KNEW ONE THING FOR SURE: IF I SURVIVED THIS, I WOULD NEVER OPEN A BOX MARKED 'TOP SECRET' EVER AGAIN. NEVER EVER.

'Honey-pot safety mechanism activated,' came the robotic bee's voice from above me.

Suddenly there was a sticky waterfall rushing past me towards the ground.

'Ahhhhhhhh,' I screamed, as I finally hit the ground.

SQUELCH AND SUCK

I waited for the pain. But it never came.

Was I paralysed already?

It took me a moment to realise I had landed in a giant pool of honey.

Phewww! Everything was all right.

Well, not everything. I didn't seem to be able to move. Not because I was hurt from the fall. Because I was stuck like a fly in a spider's web.

But other than *that*, everything was all right.

Well, actually, still not *everything*. Because just then I heard two identical blood-curdling screams. Next I saw two pairs of identical girls' shoes.

'What have you done?' the twins screamed.

'I'm not sure,' I said, because the back of my head was stuck to the **stickiest** honey ever and I couldn't see anything.

I wriggled my head backwards and forwards until it came loose and I could see what all the fuss was about.

'You've ruined our hair!' Ginger screamed.

'Oh, is that all?' I said, pleased they weren't screaming about a gigantic robotic killer bee hovering in the sky.

'And our family portraits!' Nut screeched, just as loudly as her twin.

Their hair was **drenched** in honey.

I had to admit they looked pretty terrible. And so did their paintings, which were crumpled beside them in a pool of sticky mess.

At that moment, the robotic killer bee landed silently next to us. 'Please allow me to clean your hair,' the bee said.

For the second time in a minute, Ginger and Nut screamed.

'Oh, sorry,' the droid said. 'I'm not alwayzzz shaped like a giant killer bee.'

He was obviously trying to comfort the twins, but he only caused more screaming as he transformed back into his normal droid shape.

The girls slowly backed away from us. Then they spun on their heels and ran.

Before I could even react, the droid's arm extended like a supersonic fishing rod, snapping up the twins.

'Please allow me to clean your hair,' the droid said again.

You'll never believe what happened next. A pipe extended from the droid's bum towards the girls. It looked like a giant metal snake!

Before the girls could scream yet again, the bee began suck-drying the twins' hair until the honey was all gone.

You probably haven't seen an orangutan that's used fifty cans of hairspray and twenty–four tubes of superglue. Actually, neither have I. But I'm pretty sure that's what the Ginger Nut twins now looked like!

The good news was that the girls had finally stopped screaming. They pulled their paintings out of the honey.

'You better hope this wipes off,' Nut said, rubbing at the sticky front of her canvas.

Over her shoulder, Ginger said, 'We're going to tell Mr Trunkface you were jealous of our paintings so you attacked us with some sort of crazy robotic bee . . .'

'. . . who turned into a crazy sucking robotic man,' Nut finished spitefully.

'Oh no,' I groaned.

There were **three MEGA-HECTIC PROBLEMS** here.

1. I hated to think what Mr Trunkface would do if he thought I'd tried to destroy the twins' paintings.

2. Now that the loudmouth Ginger Nut twins knew about the droid, *everyone in the world* would find out.

3. Which meant Mum was going to **DOUBLE-KILL ME . . . DEADER THAN A ZOMBIE.**

'Wait! Please!' I yelled after the twins.

'Please don't tell,' I called. 'It's a really, um, **sticky** situation!'

'Too bad, **HECTIC**,' one of them yelled back. I think it was Nut.

'Ha,' laughed the other. I think it was Ginger. 'Yeah, just because you've got a stupid silver streak in your hair doesn't mean you should mess with *our* hair. You and your robot are going to get —'

But that sentence was never finished.

The droid had transformed back into KILLER BEE mode. He swooped in from above.

With two quick jabs, he stung the Ginger Nut twins. They flopped to the ground like they had just died.

CHAPTER 5

'They will not wake for 21 minutezzz and 45 secondzzz,' said the bee.

'Phew!' I sighed with relief. 'That's great.'

I really didn't like the twins, but *killing* them would've been taking it too far.

'But it won't be so great,' I said, thinking about it some more, 'when they wake up and tell everyone.'

'The venom blankzzz memoriezzz,' the bee explained. 'In this case, they won't remember ever having seen me.'

This was back to being **great** again!

'That will be enough time to update your mother that secrecy has been **COMPROMISED**,' the bee said.

'Compromised' was a big word, but I knew what he meant. I'd failed to keep him a secret.

'But if the twins' memories of today have been wiped,' I said, 'we don't have to worry!'

'I must still inform your mother,' the robotic bee buzzed.

'Couldn't you just break the rules?' I pleaded. Telling Mum would just get us *both* into trouble.

'It izzz not possible to break the rulezzz. I am a droid. I must follow my programming.'

The funny thing was, Mum had always told me that I was programmed to *break* the rules.

It was Rule Breaker vs Rule Keeper:

THE ULTIMATE SHOWDOWN!

There was only one thing for it. I would have to wipe the droid's memory and return him to his box before Mum got home. And if I was going to do that, I was going to need **BIG FAT HELP**.

The only person in the world who could **BIG FAT HELP ME** now was my best friend Pops. He was SUPER–DUPER smart! The only problem was that he was going to take some convincing, because Pops ALWAYS got grumpy about breaking the rules.

'But I don't know how to hypnotise a droid,' Pops said again, when I told him everything that had happened. We were at the back of art class, trying to talk without Mr Trunkface hearing us. The droid had gone home, but he'd be back to pick me up after school.

I glanced over at Pops' painting. It was of him and his dad fishing in a cute little tin boat, and he was putting the finishing touches on it.

I sighed and looked at my white canvas. I had until the final bell to finish my painting. Or rather, *start* it.

Worse than that, I only had until Mum got home to clear the droid's memory.

I looked over at Pops' painting again, and thought about what Mum had said earlier.

'Just paint whatever is in your heart.'

That was the third time in a day that I had felt **THE ITCH**. This time it didn't itch in my stomach. I know it sounds pretty

SMOOSHY

but I swear, it itched at my heart.

'STRIKE ME DOWN!' I said suddenly. 'Pops, pass me the blue. I know what to paint!'

'Well, you've only got fifteen minutes,' Pops said, sounding worried, like he always did.

I think that's why Pops was my best friend. He *always* worried about me getting into **BIG FAT TROUBLE** and he *always* tried to help me get out of it (or at least make it **FAT-FREE TROUBLE**).

Basically, there was enough trouble swirling around me that he was never going to be out of a job as my best friend.

Even though his real name is Jimmy Poppolo everyone calls him Pops for short. Even his parents.

'I won't even need fifteen minutes!' I cried. 'It's the clearest vision I've ever had!'

'Here comes **HECTIC ELECTRIC!**' Pops said with a gleam in his eyes.

And that's when I painted a picture of my dad riding on a cloud surfboard in the sky. Underneath Dad, I drew me and Frenchy on my surfboard in the ocean. On the beach was Mum (still in her lab coat, because that's how Dad loved her most).

'A masterpiece, Joshie,' Mr Trunkface said as he walked by my canvas. He looked at one corner. 'And what's this? A few brushstrokes for one more person on the beach?'

I'd thought about including the droid doing something cool on the beach, like building a three-storey sandcastle. But unless Pops could hypnotise him, I'd never see him again anyway.

'Nah, I'm finished,' I said, smoothing over that section.

'Well done. I think it looks like an eleven out of ten,' Mr Trunkface said happily.

'Yes!' I cheered, with a fist pump.

Turning to the Ginger Nut twins, Mr Trunkface said, 'See what Joshie's done? This is what happens when you take care with your art.'

'Yes, Mr Trunkface,' they said in unison. They both looked really dazed.

'You're lucky the honey came off your paintings without ruining them,' he added sternly. 'But I *still* don't understand what happened.'

'We don't know, Mr Trunkface,' Ginger said.

'We can't remember,' Nut added.

'Phew,' I whispered to Pops. 'The robotic bee's venom really *did* wipe their memories!'

'You shouldn't have touched the red button in the first place,' Pops said, rolling his eyes like he always did when I was up to no good.

'I didn't,' I reminded him. **'Frenchy did.**

Now, stop grumbling like a grandpa and start thinking about how you can help me wipe the droid's memory. We'll have to get home fast after the bell rings.'

'Well, if I'm a grandpa, you must be the brainless grandkid,' Pops said, but I knew he was just joking. Then his face brightened. 'I did once hypnotise a chicken,' he said suddenly. 'A sick one.'

That got me excited. 'Isn't hypnotising and memory-wiping pretty much the same thing?'

'Well, no,' Pops said slowly. 'It's not quite the same thing. And it *might* not work.'

'Meet you at the back gate after school?

I really need your help. This has to work, Pops,' I whispered. '**Or I'm DEAD**.'

'Well, if it works then you'll be safe. If it doesn't, you'll be **DEAD** so it won't matter.' Pops grinned like it was the funniest thing ever.

'If I die, I'm going to kill you,' I told him, and then turned back to my painting.

'You two will be staying after school and writing lines,' Mr Trunkface was telling Ginger and Nut. 'Perhaps *then* you'll remember to never to come to school looking like trolls again.'

I felt a little bad because it really wasn't the twins' fault that I'd flown to school on a giant robotic killer bee and squirted them with honey and memory-wiping venom.

But just then, the twins looked over. They glared at me like they were the meanest twins in the world. It was like a small part of their brains somehow knew that I was responsible for their wild hair and memory loss. And then I remembered that they always tried to scare Frenchy. And they pulled faces at me when their dad wasn't looking. And were basically the most annoying twins in the world. So I didn't feel that bad.

Yikes, it had been a crazy day so far, and we still had a droid to hypnotise!

CHAPTER 6

'Urgh,' Pops said, as he clambered off the robotic bee and onto my balcony. 'I **never** want to do that again.'

His hair was all messed up, like the feathers of a pigeon caught in a storm.

We'd flown home on the back of the robotic bee as soon as the school bell rang, and amazingly, nothing else **HECTIC** had happened ... yet.

Frenchy was jumping up and down on my leg, but at least he wasn't stirring up **MR MOUSTACHE MAN** by barking.

'Thanks, er, Droid,' I said, sliding the balcony door shut. I shot Pops my 'you'd better be ready to work your genuis' look.

Pops and I had a plan to erase the droid's memory by hypnotising him. Then we could put him back into the box before Mum got home. The hard part would be doing it without the droid *knowing* what we were up to.

'So, uh, Droid. Is it true that you can become any animal in the world?' Pops asked.

'I am programmed to shape-shift into approximately 4 billion different shapes.'

'Could you become a chicken?' Pops asked innocently. 'Like, now?'

'Initiating Kentucky Unfried Chicken mode,' said the droid, and began to shape-shift.

His arms bent at the elbows and transformed into the wings of a chicken. As the wings flapped down and then up, I could see a factory of gears and cogs spinning in his blue joints. Each new click of the cogs made another feather sprout.

KENTUCKY UNFRIED CHICKEN MODE

SUPER-DELUXE PILLOW-GRADE FEATHERS

BULLET-PROOF BODY ARMOUR

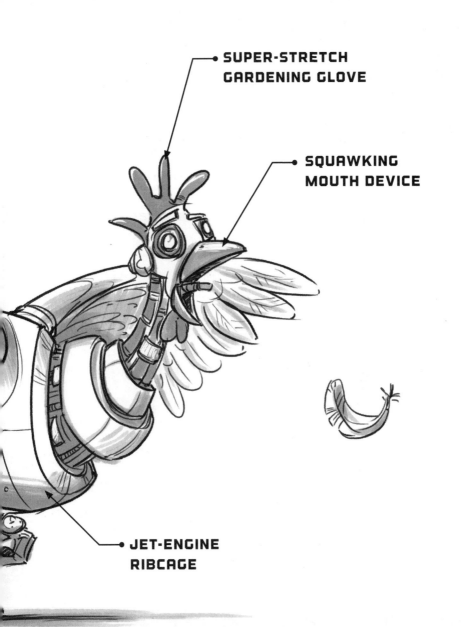

SUPER-STRETCH GARDENING GLOVE

SQUAWKING MOUTH DEVICE

JET-ENGINE RIBCAGE

'Yes!' I hissed. 'Pops, you're the **BOMB**.'

'Your mother will be home soon,' the robotic chicken clucked. 'I will prepare my update for her now. Please give me 1 minute and 33 seconds to do this. My programs are running slower while in chicken mode.'

'Ummmm, okay,' I said.

His eyes glazed over as he went offline. Man, it looked like he was preparing a big update for Mum.

I was beginning to feel nervous. Time was running out. If Mum found out that I'd disobeyed her by opening the box, AND that her **TOP SECRET** project had been seen

by the Ginger Nut twins, it would be the end
of my entire world!

'Now what?' I whispered to Pops.

'Last time, I stroked the chicken's head,'
Pops whispered back.

'Well, do it now while he's distracted,' I said.

Pops started stroking the robotic chicken,
but nothing happened. 'Then I moved my
finger from side to side in front of the
chicken's face, like this,' he added, moving his
finger from left to right (in case that wasn't
obvious).

After he had been stroking the chicken and
waving his hand in front of it for a few minutes,

Pops whispered, 'I don't think it's working.'

'But you've done this before!' I said

desperately. 'What's different?'

'Other than him being a robotic chicken?'

Pops said. 'Oh, and maybe that he's not sick.'

'STRIKE ME DOWN!'

I exclaimed. 'That's it!' I had an idea. It had

to work. Because I was **DEADER**

THAN DEAD if it didn't.

I flung open the fridge and took out Mum's

leftover vegan stew.

'What are you doing?' Pops asked, gagging

when I opened the plastic container.

'This smells worse than a dog's fart that's

been farting,' I said. My friend's eyes went wide, but for once he didn't look worried. He just pinched his nose and grinned at me.

Frenchy barked at me. Like I said, I don't speak French but I was pretty sure he was saying that not even **HIS** farts smelt that bad.

'Are you back online?' I asked the droid.

'Please wait 8.45 seconds.'

'I just want to see if you can eat human food,' I said, when the light in the droid-chicken's eyes flicked on.

'A droid can eat anything,' he said. 'But food is not transformed into energy like it is in humans.'

'Try this,' I said, holding my nose. Carefully – **CAREFULLY** – I put the stinky container of vegan stew on the ground.

The droid-chicken pecked at the stew, just like a real chicken pecks at food. At first, nothing happened.

But a few minutes later, the droid-chicken started wobbling on his clawy chicken feet.

His feathers started drooping and then shaking and then . . .

POOF

The droid-chicken's feathers flew off his mechanical wings, right in our faces!

Frenchy snapped at the floating feathers in delight. He started barking.

There were feathers everywhere! It was like Pops and I had just had a pillow fight, right there in the kitchen.

But Frenchy's barking was getting out of control.

'Shhhhh,' I shout-whispered at him.

But he paid me no notice. This was bad. His barking was going to ...

THUMP
THUMP
THUMP

. . . set off **MR MOUSTACHE MAN!**

CHAPTER 7

Oh no. *This* was getting **HECTIC!**

'WHAT'S GOING ON IN THERE?' a voice

thundered from outside our apartment.

'Ummmm,' I said.

Because how do you explain the noise

made by a French bulldog chasing the feathers of a gigantic robotic chicken who's feeling sick after eating Mum's vegan stew?

'Sorry,' I called, 'Frenchy saw a chicken on YouTube and went crazy!'

'YOUTUBE BAHHHH,' he shouted through the apartment door. **'DON'T YOU KIDS GET GIVEN HOMEWORK THESE DAYS? THIS IS YOUR SECOND WARNING THIS WEEK. ONE MORE WARNING AND THAT DOG WILL HAVE TO GO!'**

The feathers had stopped falling, which meant Frenchy stopped barking. *Finally.*

'We're watching *Worst Cat Stacks* now, so Frenchy's calmed down,' I shouted, but there was no answer. **MR MOUSTACHE MAN** must have gone off in a huff.

'W-h-a-a-a-t h-a-p-p-e-n-e-d?' the now featherless robotic chicken asked slowly, in a voice that sounded like he needed charging.

'We've done it,' I whispered to Pops. To the robotic chicken, I said, 'I think Mum's vegan stew has made you sick.'

'Negative. I am not "sick" as you might say in human terms,' the droid-chicken clucked. 'But my core programming does seem to have a virus.'

Yep, even the best artificial intelligence in the world can't eat Mum's vegan stew.

'Well, Pops is an expert in curing sick chickens,' I said. 'He's going to help get rid of your virus.'

The robotic chicken nodded weakly. 'Thank you. I am finding it hard to compute what is happening.'

'Do your thing,' I said, winking at Pops.

And that's when Pops started hypnotising the droid to wipe his memory for real. He rubbed the robotic chicken's head. He even did some weird flapping movements, like he was imitating a chicken trying to fly.

And, finally, he held his finger in front of the chicken's eyes and slowly moved it from left to right.

The robotic chicken kept watching Pops' hand swing from side to side. The rest of him was totally still. Before we knew it, the featherless robotic chicken was lying, as stiff as a board, on the floor.

'SYSTEM SHUT·DOWN,' announced a slow computerised voice from within the droid.

'You're a total genius, Pops!' I cried.

What a best friend. **FAT-FREE TROUBLE** was finally coming my way!

Pops grinned and we jumped up for our special 'air-high-five' over the top of the unconscious droid-chicken lying on my kitchen floor.

'So, is his memory wiped?' I asked.

Pops bit his lip, and then shook his head. 'Honestly,

I'm not sure. Hypnotising him only really puts him to sleep. If he's like any normal computer, his memory chip will be totally fine.'

I nodded. Yep. There was still a little bit of trouble left!

But ...

I had a feeling I knew *exactly* what had to be done.

It was going to be **totally gross**. I hope you don't get that case of **SSP (SUDDEN SICK PANTS)** that I warned you about before.

'We've only got one option left,' I said, pushing up the sleeve of my hoodie. 'I'm going to find his memory chip. Wish me luck!'

'Oh no,' Pops said, a look of horror on his face. 'Don't do it!'

He knew exactly what I was thinking.

Or should I say, he knew exactly what I was *stinking*!

Either I had to do one of the **GROSSEST** things ever, or my droid would be turned into scrap metal.

I stopped.

Did you notice that I just said *my droid*? We'd only had one crazy day together, but already the droid felt like he was *mine*. Like I'd miss him if he were gone.

Like perhaps he was already more to me than just a droid.

And that's when I put my finger up the robotic-chicken's bum.

'Yuuuuuuuckkkkkkkkk!' Pops said, his face scrunching up like he'd just eaten ten sherbet bombs and five lemons at the same time.

'You're telling me,' I muttered to Pops as I moved my fingers around, searching for something that could be a memory chip.

I can tell you, it wasn't pleasant.

No one wants to put their hand inside a chicken's bum, even a robotic one. And this was no ordinary-sized robotic chicken. My arm was in all the way up to my elbow. I was feeling through all sorts of cables and electrical pieces.

I finally pulled my hand out from

deep inside the bottom of the world's most

powerful artificially intelligent robotic chicken

'Wow, **HECTIC**,' Pops said. 'That was

awesome. Gross, but awesome.'

In my hand was the memory chip.

CHAPTER 8

'You didn't open the box, did you?' Mum asked, the moment she put her briefcase down on the kitchen bench.

'Ummm no,' I said, trying not to look at Frenchy. **'I didn't.'**

Thankfully Frenchy was lying in his little bed next to the balcony. He was tuckered out from all that feather-catching.

'Good, because we'd both be in *deep trouble* with the government if anyone found out about this,' she said. 'And I wanted to take you through the safety procedures first.'

Yikes. I had my fingers, toes and even my eyes crossed, hoping that I had wiped the droid's memory.

The funny thing was, another part of me felt sad that my droid would never remember our first day together. There it is — I said it again. *My* droid.

Mum looked over at me. 'Can you guess what's inside?'

I shook my head.

'Press that button,' she told me, pointing.

For the first time — *officially* — I pressed the red button, and a giant robotic chicken flew out of the box.

'STRIKE ME DOWN!' I yelled.

Even I hadn't been expecting the robotic **chicken** again!

'That's not supposed to happen!' Mum said as feathers went flying. 'It's meant to be your new babysitter.'

'Cool, Mum. A robotic chicken for a

babysitter. Dad always said you were full of crazy ideas, but this is next level . . .'

'Hang on, Joshie,' she said. 'Commence DAD mode.'

The robotic chicken began to shift back into its normal shape. But instead of stopping at his droid form, he continued to change into something totally different again.

In an instant, my heart stopped beating. He didn't look like the droid from today anymore. But that's not what stopped my heart.

'Excellent,' Mum said, in her matter-of-fact way. 'Looks like it's fully operational.'

My scalp had gone cold. 'You've got to be joking,' I said quietly. I could hardly look at the droid standing before me. I could feel tears pouring down my face like someone had left the garden hose on behind my eyes. And I didn't even care that I was crying.

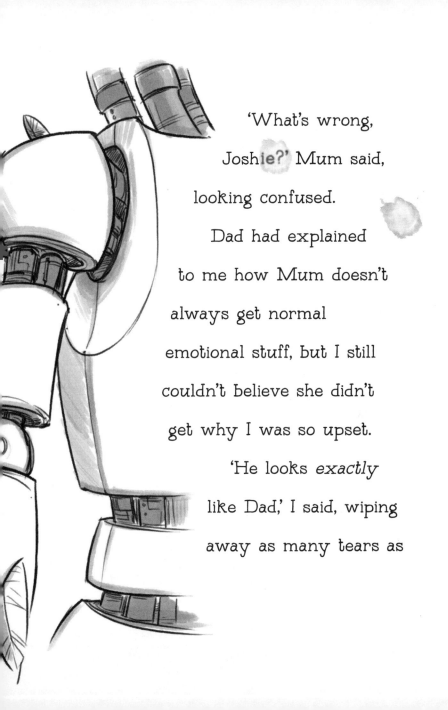

'What's wrong, Joshie?' Mum said, looking confused. Dad had explained to me how Mum doesn't always get normal emotional stuff, but I still couldn't believe she didn't get why I was so upset.

'He looks *exactly* like Dad,' I said, wiping away as many tears as

I could with the back of my hand.

'I know,' Mum said, as if it were the happiest thought she'd ever had. 'It'll be like having him with us again!'

'No way. I'll run away from home if you don't change him!' I shouted. There was **no way** this droid was replacing my dad.

Mum tried to hug me but I turned away.

'Perhaps you're right,' Mum said. 'Should we give him grey hair and a walking stick?'

I shook my head, sniffling just a little bit. 'Nah. He just needs to be … can we please just make him **COOL?**'

'What's cool?' Mum asked.

I sometimes forget Mum is a geeky scientist.

'I don't know. Just make him a dude, Mum.'

Mum shrugged. 'Well, we can give it a go! Go into Droid Dude mode,' she commanded.

'That's it,' I said, wiping my eyes one last time. I liked the idea of a DROID DUDE.

'Yes, ma'am,' the droid said.

Wild hair sprouted on his head. It was the color of a caramel milkshake. His skin went from white to super-tanned, like he had spent all summer surfing.

From out of his body, thousands of tiny sewing-machine nanobots started sewing clothes on him.

First, a pair of Hawaiian boardshorts appeared. Then a T-shirt that had 'Break The Rules If You Want' written on it. And finally, a pair of bright yellow thongs grew on his huge feet.

Frenchy was up now, his tail wagging. Droid Dude looked like the coolest surfer ever.

'Hmmmmm,' Mum said. 'If he's going to look after you, I think we should make him look a little bit more like a grown-up. Please add a moustache to DROID DUDE mode,' she said, to update the droid's programming.

Even though I'd seen the droid shape-shift, it made me giggle when I saw him grow a big bushy moustache in less than ten seconds!

'Moustache complete,' the droid told us.

'What do you think?' Mum asked me.

'No way,' I said. 'It reminds me of **MR MOUSTACHE MAN.'**

'Fine then,' Mum said, 'as long as you listen to him when he's checking on your homework. Otherwise, the moustache is back.'

We both laughed. 'Cancel moustache,' I commanded, and it disappeared just as quickly. I gave Mum a big hug. I didn't even mind all her pens pressing into my ear.

I looked over at our pretty cool droid, and remembered I had his memory chip in my pocket. I still felt a bit sad that he wouldn't remember our first adventure together.

Just then, a grinding noise came from the droid. 'What's that?' Mum asked, raising an eyebrow.

'Back-up memory,' the droid said.

'That's strange,' said Mum. 'There shouldn't be anything to remember yet.'

I went very still, absolutely **CERTAIN** that I was **BUSTED**.

But the droid just looked back at her. 'An old file,' he explained.

And I swear, when Mum wasn't looking, he **winked** at me.

THE END

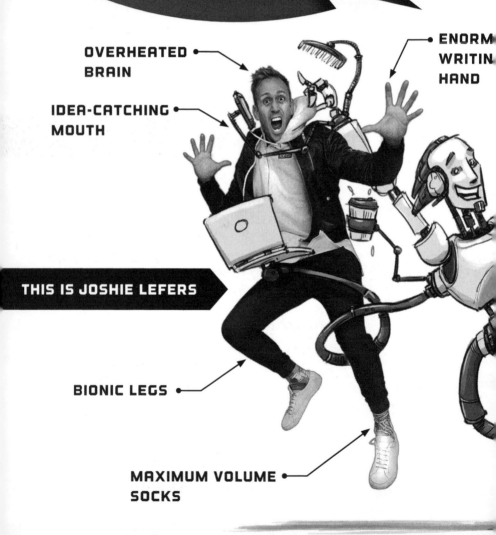

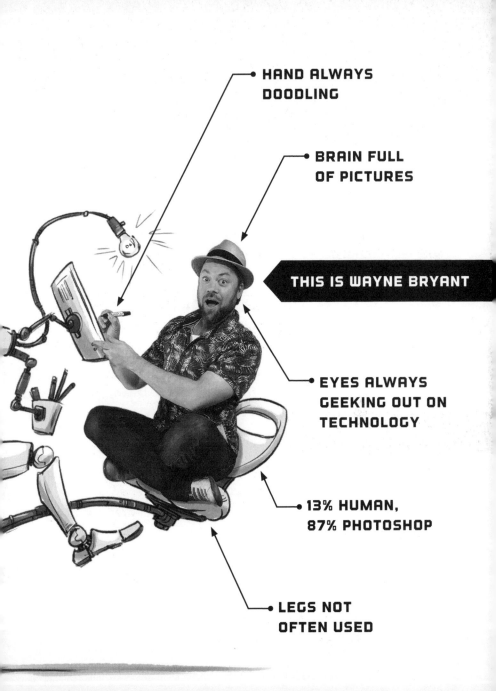

HAND ALWAYS DOODLING

BRAIN FULL OF PICTURES

THIS IS WAYNE BRYANT

EYES ALWAYS GEEKING OUT ON TECHNOLOGY

13% HUMAN, 87% PHOTOSHOP

LEGS NOT OFTEN USED

ACKNOWLEDGEMENTS

Hilary Rogers — you are the Electric to my Hectic that made this book and series come to life. Your magic touch is across every page. As one of Australia's most accomplished talents in creating kids' book series, there's no one in the world I could be as fortunate to work with. Thank you forever and beyond!

Penny White, Marisa Pintado, Annabel Barker, Kate Brown, Ilka Tulloch, Pooja Desai, Luna Soo and the rest of you champions at Hardie Grant Egmont — we've ended up becoming quite the team! Thank you all so much (and especially you, Pen) for going after this series. It's you guys that make it possible for us authors to do our thing. You have my endless admiration and gratitude.

Antoni Jach — my wonderful friend, thanks times a gazillion for helping me to become a published author! And on behalf of countless writers, thanks for making our lives so rich. I salute you, legend.

Sally Rippin — your amazing contribution to kids' books seems boundless. Thanks for the super sessions, and for helping make Joshie be Joshie!

Wayne Bryant – if it was funny when I wrote it, it became even funnier when you illustrated it.

Jarett Lefers – bro, you're a genius, my best friend and greatest inspiration. You've helped make every day a better alternative reality than the last.

Johan Lefers – Dad, what can I say? Your boundless energy and creativity has inspired me all my life. Without the glee of Lord Itchy Bum, there couldn't have been Hectic Electric.

Jutka Lefers – Mum, you taught me to go after whatever I wanted in life. Love you so much.

Jasmin Lefers – you'll be my naughty Bread Baby sister soon. Thanks for the inspiration and for all your love.

Sarah Roberts – my soul soars when I think of you and your unflagging belief in me and in my writing. Thank you, beautiful girl.

Emma and Rachel – thanks for being the inspiration for the Ginger Nut Twins. (And Deb, you created beautiful girls, and I turned them into bullies!)

Stephen Wools – you're the best partner in crime I could hope for! It's been years of creative epicness together! Here's to many more.

What could **possibly** go wrong when Joshie decides to get Droid Dude to bake him a robotic gingerbread sister? Read **THE RISE OF THE BREAD BABY** to find out!

HECTIC ELECTRIC

THE RISE OF THE JOSHIE LEFERS
BREAD BABY

ART BY WAYNE BRYANT